This Walker book belongs to:

_____

_____

_____

For Nana

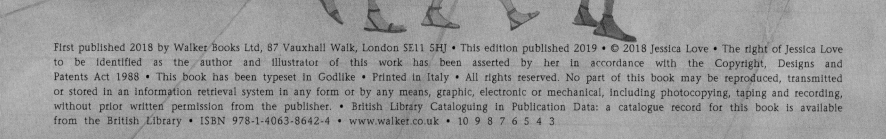

First published 2018 by Walker Books Ltd, 87 Vauxhall Walk, London SE11 5HJ • This edition published 2019 • © 2018 Jessica Love • The right of Jessica Love to be identified as the author and illustrator of this work has been asserted by her in accordance with the Copyright, Designs and Patents Act 1988 • This book has been typeset in Godlike • Printed in Italy •
• British Library Cataloguing in Publication Data: a catalogue record for this book is available from the British Library • ISBN 978-1-4063-8642-4 • www.walker.co.uk • 10 9 8 7 6 5 4 3

JULIAN IS A MERMAID

Jessica Love

WALKER BOOKS
AND SUBSIDIARIES

LONDON • BOSTON • SYDNEY • AUCKLAND

This is a boy named Julian. And this is his Nana.
And those are some mermaids.

Julian LOVES mermaids.

"Let's go, honey. This is our stop."

"Nana, did you see the mermaids?"

"I saw them, honey."

"Nana, I am also a mermaid."

"I'm going to take a bath. You be good."

Julian has an idea.

"Oh!"

"Come here, honey."

"For me, Nana?"

"For you, Julian."

"Where are we going?"

"You'll see," says Nana.

"*Mermaids,*" whispers Julian.

"Like you, honey. Let's join them."

And they do.

"A bravura feat of understated storytelling" *Guardian*

"Readers learn that anyone can be a mermaid: All it takes is love and acceptance, a little imagination and a big swishy tail" *The New York Times*

"This creatively told book does a great job of dismantling gender stereotypes" *Evening Standard*

"A celebration of being yourself ... exudes warmth and joy" *The Scotsman*

"A lesson in self-love for all ages!" *Pride magazine*

"Utterly gorgeous ... great for questioning our gender stereotypes but without being at all preachy" *Sun*

"Magnificent children's picture book" *RuPaul*

"So sweet" *Neil Gaiman*

"Probably my favourite book ever illustrated. To think that this is going to be a book that kids are reading makes my heart beat even faster and harder" *Laura Dockrill*